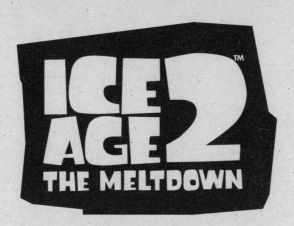

ICE AGE 2
THE MELTDOWN

THE MOVIE NOVEL

D0721211

HarperCollins®, 🖛®, and HarperKidsEntertainment™
are trademarks of HarperCollins Publishers.

ICE AGE 2: THE MOVIE NOVEL

Ice Age 2 The Meltdown™ & © 2006 Twentieth Century Fox Film Corporation.
For information address HarperCollins Children's Books, a division of HarperCollins Publishers,
1350 Avenue of the Americas, New York, NY 10019.
www.harperchildrens.com
www.iceage2.com
Library of Congress catalog card number: 2005936331
ISBN-10: 0-06-083974-0—ISBN-13: 978-0-06-083974-1
Book design by Joe Merkel
1 2 3 4 5 6 7 8 9 10
❖
First Edition

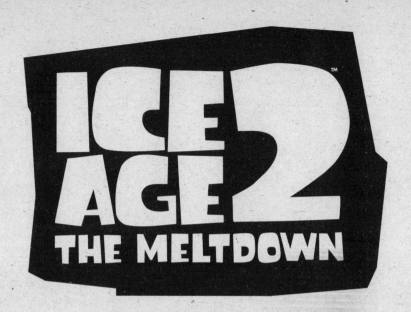

THE MOVIE NOVEL

BY KATHLEEN WEIDNER ZOEHFELD

HarperKidsEntertainment
An Imprint of HarperCollinsPublishers

CHAPTER 1

SID'S SUMMER CAMP

The warm sun glinted on the sheer white sides of the glacier as pretty blue waterfalls trickled down the side of them. In the valley below, a boisterous group of baby animals splashed happily in the little pools. Every summer, the animals flocked to this sparkling valley. The glacier's slopes and fissures made the best waterslides for miles around.

High above the crowd, using his claws as ice picks, a wild-eyed prehistoric squirrel scaled the glacier. He stabbed the tip of the overhang with his teeth and hoisted himself up on top of the glacier to seize his prize: an acorn he had buried months ago. *Pop!* He pulled the nut out of the ice. Water shot out of the hole and splashed him in the eye. The little Scrat poked his finger in the hole to stop the leak.

Crrrrrraaaaaaaaaakkkkkk! Pop! The glacier sprang another leak. And then another! What had he done? The Scrat struggled desperately to stop the leaks. He tried using his snout like a cork. But the water gushed into his mouth, filling him up like a big water balloon.

Pssssshhh!!! The force of the water shot him off the glacier like a rocket, and he sailed over the animals' heads. No one below noticed the flying Scrat. Especially not Sid the sloth, who had his paws full, hopelessly trying to contain the animal kids who had just been let loose to bask in the freedom of summer camp.

Two rambunctious aardvark kids chased each other across the beach and trampled a little beaver's sand castle under their feet. The little beaver wailed.

Sid noticed that one of the prettiest sloths in the valley was looking in his direction. Trying to act the part of a real lifeguard, he raised his shell whistle to his lips and blew. "No running, James!" he ordered. "Camp rules!"

"Bite me, sloth!" cried James. The hefty aardvark kid ran right past Sid at top speed and did a cannonball into the kiddie pool.

"Bite me, *sir*," corrected Sid. He glanced at the pretty sloth. "It's all about respect," he explained.

She rolled her eyes scornfully as she strode away.

Completely out of control, Sid barked out orders. "Jared, you just ate. Wait an hour! Hector, no, no, no, you can't pee-pee there. Okay, there is fine. Ashley, stop picking your noooooooooo . . . !"

A bunch of kids grabbed him by the tail, and before he knew it he was dangling upside down from a branch.

"Yay! Piñata!" cheered the kids.

Someone whacked him with a big stick.

"Stop!" Sid shouted. "You're supposed to wear blindfolds."

"You're in no position to make the rules," said a snippy little beaver girl.

"Hey, it's my turn to hit the sloth," cried James.

"My turn! My turn!" yelled the kids, fighting over who would be next to swing. *Whack! Whack! Whack!*

"*Whoaahhhhhhhhhh!*" cried Sid, as he fell to the ground with a thud.

"Hey, you didn't have any candy in you," complained the beaver girl.

"Not even a little!" whined Sid.

"Let's bury him!" shouted another voice from the crowd.

"*Yeaaaaahhhhhh!*"

A few husky glyptodon kids dug a hole in the ground, while the others dragged Sid toward it.

Boing! Boing! Boing! The kids stamped the dirt down around his body and bounced on his head.

"Ow, ow, ow!" he cried.

Suddenly James had another idea: "Fire ants!"

"*Yeaaaaahhhhhh!*"

But a big booming voice interrupted their wild cheers. "What is going on here?"

The kids froze in their tracks.

"And how can we make it more painful?" added another, even scarier voice.

Putting on their most wide-eyed, innocent-looking faces, the kids stared up at the two imposing creatures who had just arrived. It was Manfred, Sid's mammoth pal, and their fierce saber-toothed tiger friend, Diego.

"Manny! Diego!" cried Sid in relief. "My bad mammal jammals! Wanna give a sloth a hand?"

Manny used his elephantine trunk to pull Sid out of the hole.

"Look!" exclaimed Sid, as he brushed the dirt off his green fur. "I opened my camp—*Campo del Sid!* Catchy, huh? It means Camp of Sid."

"Congratulations," growled Diego. "Now you are an idiot in two languages."

"Not in front of the K-I-D-Z," whispered Sid. "These guys love me. Right, Billy?"

"Don't make me eat you," the little rhino replied.

"They kid," cried Sid. "That's why they're called kids."

"I told you, Sid. You're not qualified to run a summer camp," said Manny.

"Oh, since when do qualifications have anything to do with child care?" Sid sulked. "Besides, these kids look up to me. I'm a role model to them."

As he was saying this, two beaver kids wrapped vines around his legs and pushed him over.

"Oh yeah, I can see that," said Diego.

"You guys never think I can do anything. I'm an equal member of this herd, you know. So you need to start treating me with respect!" Sid hopped away with his legs still tied together.

Manny and Diego glanced over their shoulders at the mischievous crowd of youngsters.

"Hey, let's play pin the tail on the mammoth!" cried the beaver girl.

"*Yeaaaaahhhhhh!*"

Yikes! Manny and Diego exchanged a worried look. "Sid, we were kidding. Come back here!" they called.

But Sid was already halfway across the water park. He had wiggled his way out of the vines and was storming off bravely toward the highest, twistiest, most treacherous waterslide in the valley.

By the time Sid steeled himself for the steep ascent up the glacier, Manny and Diego had finally begun to establish some order at the summer camp.

Manny decided to tell the kids a story about a little burro and his mommy. Everyone listened with rapt attention.

" . . . and so, in the end, the little burro reached his mommy. And they lived happily ever after," he concluded.

The kids cheered and applauded.

Diego gave Manny a nod of approval.

But the order didn't last for long. The kids began squirming and raising their hands with questions.

"Why does the burro go home? Why doesn't he stay with the rabbits?" asked one of the beaver boys.

"Because he wanted to be with his family," answered Manny.

"I think he should go with the girl burro. That's a better love story," declared a bird.

"Okay, well, when you tell your burro story, that's what he'll do," agreed Manny.

"Burro is a demeaning name," said Oscar the glyptodon. "Technically it's called a 'wild ass.'"

"YEAH!!!"

"Fine," declared Manny. "The wild ass boy came home to his wild ass mother."

The kids fell over laughing.

Manny scowled. "That's why I called it a burro!"

"Could the burro have a grazing problem?" asked a young rhino. "That would make him more relatable."

"Bor-ing," commented one of the aardvarks.

"It's not believable," declared a beaver boy.

"Do burros eat their young?" asked Billy.

"It's not a very satisfying ending," complained the beaver girl.

"Sometimes I throw up," declared a start girl, out of the blue.

Manny was losing patience. "They lived happily ever after!" he cried. "You can't get more satisfying than that! One big happy family! That's the way it's supposed to be."

The young bird girl cocked her head and stared at him. "Then where's your big happy family?"

The question hit Manny like a ton of bricks. He stood there speechless, lost in his own sad thoughts.

"Then the hungry tiger ate the pesky little kids!" roared Diego, coming to Manny's rescue. He made mock lunges at the kids and shooed them away.

"You okay, buddy?" he asked when they were gone.

The big mammoth shrugged off his friend's concern. "Sure. Why not?"

"I just thought you . . ."

"Storytime's over. The end!" cried Manny. He turned and walked away.

CHAPTER 2

THE END OF THE WORLD

All Manny wanted was a little time alone to think. But he and Diego were soon distracted by a strange, low rumbling sound in the distance. Before they knew it, hundreds of panicky animals were packing up their things and hurrying out of the water park.

"Where's everybody going?" asked Diego.

"The world's coming to an end!" shouted a tapir, as he trotted past.

"What are you talking about?" cried Manny.

"Fast Tony, he says the world's going to flood!" yelled the tapir.

Fast Tony was a shady, fast-talking armadillo. Manny and Diego found him giving a sales pitch to a crowd of animals. At his feet was a pile of useless-looking reeds.

"Folks, I hold in my hand a device so powerful, it can actually pull air right out of the sky," he declared, holding up one of the flimsy, hollow stalks.

An aardvark woman listened attentively.

"Do you have gills, ma'am?" Fast Tony asked her. She shook her head "no."

"So you can't breathe underwater?"

"Nuh-uh."

"Ah-ha! Then allow my assistant here to demonstrate."

Fast Tony handed the reed to his sidekick, a slow-witted glyptodon named Stu.

Stu stuck the thing up his nose. "Hey, I can smell the ocean!" he declared.

Fast Tony grabbed the reed back in annoyance.

"What are you doing? I can't sell that now!" he cried. "You suck air through your mouth, you moron!" He shoved the tube in Stu's mouth and dunked his head in a puddle.

Fast Tony turned back to the crowd and continued his sales pitch. "So, its tasteful design and sturdy construction mean you'll have plenty of air for eons to come. . . ."

Manny moved in, scooped up the shifty armadillo with his trunk, and dangled him in the air.

"Hey!" cried Fast Tony.

"Why are you scaring everyone with this doomsday stuff?" Manny demanded.

Fast Tony gave the audience a sheepish laugh. Then he scowled at Manny and whispered, "I'm trying to make a living here, pal." He rolled himself up into a ball and bounced back to the ground. "It's all part of my accu-weather forecast. The five-day outlook is calling for intense flooding followed by the end of the world . . . with a slight chance of patchy sunshine later in the week."

The animals were growing more alarmed by the minute.

"Don't listen to him," Manny told them. "Fast

Tony would sell his own mother for a grape."

"Are you making an offer? I mean . . . no, I would not!" cried Fast Tony, faking indignation.

"But haven't you heard? The ice is melting!" cried an aardvark.

"See this ground?" said Manny. "It's covered in ice. A thousand years ago it was covered in ice. A thousand years from now it will *still be ice*!"

One of the aardvark dads stepped up. "Say, buddy, not to cast aspersions on your survival instincts or nothing, but haven't mammoths pretty much gone extinct?"

"What are you talking about?" demanded Manny.

"I'm talking about *you* being the last of your kind," he replied.

"Ah, your breath smells like ants," said Manny dismissively.

The aardvark stuck his nose in his mouth to check and cringed in embarrassment. His breath did smell like ants! "Be that as it may," he said, regaining his dignity, "when's the last time you saw another mammoth?"

"Don't pay attention to him, Manny," said Diego.

"Mammoths can't go extinct," said Manny.

"They're the biggest things on earth!"

"What about the dinosaurs?" asked one of the beaver moms.

"The dinosaurs got cocky," grumbled Manny. "They made enemies."

Suddenly a freaky-looking little mammal pointed to the glacier and cried, "Look, some idiot's going down the Evicerator!"

Everyone looked up at the death-defying glacier, except Manny. "Please tell me it's not our idiot," he moaned to Diego.

High atop the glittering glacier a familiar little furry creature was waving his arms shouting, "I'm gonna jump on the count of three! One . . . two . . ."

"Sid! Don't move a muscle. We're coming up!" yelled Manny.

"Jump! Jump! Jump!" chanted the malicious crowd.

"Jump. Jump," muttered Diego.

Manny shot him a look.

"Sorry," he said softly.

By the time Manny and Diego reached the top, Sid was standing there, petrified and still counting: " . . . two and three one thousandths, two and four one thousandths . . ."

"Sid! What are you doing!? Get down from there!" cried Manny.

"No way!" cried Sid. "I'm gonna be the first to jump off the Eviscerator. Then you guys are gonna have to start showing me some respect."

"You jump off this, the only respect you're gonna get is respect for the dead," warned Manny.

"Come on," said Diego. "He's not that stupid."

Sid tucked into position for the slide.

"But I've been wrong before," Diego added.

"*Geronimo!*" cried Sid as he plummeted off the edge.

Manny reached out over the icy precipice with his trunk and caught Sid in midair. Thrown off balance by the catch, Manny teetered and stumbled backwards into Diego, sending him sliding across a wet slick of ice. Then Manny toppled over. *Kerplop!* Right on top of Sid!

"I . . . can't . . . breathe," gasped Sid, poking his head out from under Manny's massive bulk. "I think I just coughed up my spleen."

As they righted themselves, they realized they had fallen onto a wide frozen lake. And the ice was very thin. As Diego padded back toward them, cracks began to form around his paws wherever he took a step. He could see bubbles moving just under the surface.

The ice was giving way! He made a desperate dash for safety. As one last crack snapped and boomed behind him, he leaped toward Manny and attached himself to the mammoth's nose as if it were the trunk of a tree.

"Diego," Manny groaned, "retract . . . the . . . claws!"

Diego dropped to the ground, still hyper-ventilating. "Oh, right . . . sorry. . ."

"If I didn't know you better, Diego, I'd think you were afraid of the water," taunted Sid.

Diego grabbed the sloth by the throat and eyeballed him threateningly.

"Okay, good thing I know you better," Sid squeaked.

Sid hurried to Manny's side. The mammoth was gazing out over the wide expanse of ice with a stunned expression on his face. The whole lake had begun to thaw! And the glacier they were standing on was the only thing holding all that water back.

The three friends turned and looked out across

their valley. All of the huge glaciers that surrounded the valley had lakes behind them, just like this one.

"Fast Tony was right," said Manny. "Everything's melting. It's all gonna flood." He gazed at the youngsters who had gone back to frolicking in the water park below. "C'mon, we've got to warn them!"

"Maybe we can very rapidly evolve into water creatures," suggested Sid.

"That's genius, Sid," said Diego.

"Just call me 'Squid!'"

As they traversed a narrow bridge of ice, Sid easily broke off a piece. "Jeez, this whole thing's a piece of junk. I can't believe I live here."

Crrrrraaaaaaakkkkk! The ice began to collapse!

Diego and Manny shot Sid an accusing look.

"What?"

Before they could answer, the whole shelf of ice crumbled beneath them and sent them flying willy-nilly down the dreaded Eviscerator.

As the mammals shot down the gorge, Fast Tony continued his sales pitch below.

"Forget reeds! That is so five minutes ago! I present you with this revolutionary gizmo we call, 'bark'! It's so buoyant, it actually floats!" he shouted.

Manny, Sid, and Diego skimmed across the surface of a pool like three skipping stones and crashed—*Whop! Smash! Kablam!*—into Fast Tony's podium.

Fast Tony curled up in a ball to protect himself.

"See!?" he cried, slowly uncurling after they had settled down. "This is what I'm talking about! Giant balls of furry lava, the size of mammoths, raining from the sky."

"Ah, go suck air through a reed!" cried a grumpy old beaver.

"Hey, Fast Tony!" taunted the tapir. "The snakes called. They want their oil back."

Nobody believed Fast Tony anymore! Manny regretted that he had convinced the animals they had nothing to fear. "You've got to listen to him!" he cried. "He's right about the flood."

"I am . . . ? I mean, yes. I am," declared Fast Tony.

"Wait. You said there wasn't going to be a flood. Why should we listen to you?" asked a skeptical elk.

"Because we saw what's up there!" cried Manny. "The dams are gonna break! The entire valley's gonna flood!"

The crowd just laughed in his face.

"Flood's real alright. And it's comin' fast," said a voice from above.

The crowd looked around to see where the voice was coming from. The source was a vulture perched in a tree branch.

"Look around. You're in a bowl. This bowl's gonna fill up fast. Ain't no way out."

The crowd started to panic. Quiet murmurs could be heard as the animals turned to one another with fearful eyes. The vulture interrupted the crowd with his assured tone.

"Unless . . . you can make it to the end of the valley. There's a boat. It can save you. And it's real, I've seen it myself," the vulture said.

The crowd breathed a sigh of relief and relaxed. An aardvark dad sat down on a log.

"But ya'll better hurry," the vulture continued. "Valley's changin' into a savage beast. Ground's meltin', walls tumblin', rocks crumblin'. In three days' time—*BOOM!*"

The animals gasped.

"There is some good news, though."

The animals gave the vulture a hopeful look.

"The more of you die, the better I eat."

The animals trembled in fear.

"I didn't say it was good news for you," quipped the vulture as he flapped his big, ugly wings and took off over the valley.

"Ew, he must've been a pleasure to have in class," said Sid sarcastically.

"Alright, you heard the scary vulture. Let's move out!" ordered Manny.

CHAPTER 3

WATER REPTILES!

Just as the vulture vanished over the horizon, an enormous chunk of the glacier broke off and came rumbling and tumbling down into the water park. The animals fled in terror.

The giant ice boulder crashed into a deep pool. Manny thought he could see something strange inside. But the ice was cloudy, and Diego hurried him away. "Manny, let's go!" he cried.

The three pals made their way out of the valley, just behind the rest of the animals. Not one of them noticed two huge, mysterious forms thawing out of the ice and slowly coming to life. The fleeing herd of animals was too busy pushing and shoving, forming a bottleneck in the narrow passage that led out of the park.

Two old vultures hovered overhead like helicopter pilots doing the nightly traffic report.

"We got an overturned glyptodon in the far right lane. Traffic backed up as far as the eye can see," said one.

"It looks like there's a fatality," cried the other.

"Mmmmmm . . . I want the dark meat!" squawked the first. Forgetting all about the report, they swooped down for the treat.

The animals were frantic to escape the flood and avoid the looming vultures.

"C'mon! Let's go! Come, come, come. Get in," clucked a mother bird, herding her chicks into their nest. Once they were inside, she scooped up the nest and ran.

Nearby, a family of mole hogs desperately tried to

coax their old grandpa out of his hole. They grabbed his tail and pulled. "C'mon, Grandpa! We have to go!" they all shouted.

"Well, I'm not leaving!" Grandpa shouted back. "I was born in this hole. And I'll die in this hole!"

A dung beetle family rushed past, each one pushing a big dung-ball several times its size.

"Do we have to bring this crap?" complained the dad. "I'm sure there's more crap where we're going."

"This was a gift from my mother!" cried the mom beetle.

Manny shook his head in dismay. He tried to get the migration flowing smoothly. "Keep it moving!" he ordered.

Sid trotted up, stuffing berries in his mouth, and lisped, "Manny, I jusht heard you're going ex-shtinct."

"I am not going extinct," replied Manny.

"Oh . . . well, if you do go extinct, can I have your spot on the food chain?" The green fur around his mouth was turning purple from the dripping berry juice.

"Hey! If you ever master hygiene, try working on sensitivity," Diego scolded.

"What part of 'not going extinct' do you not understand?" asked Manny.

"I'm having trouble with the 'not' part," said Sid. "I think you are, too."

"I told you, I'm not going extinct!" shouted Manny.

"Kids! Look! The last mammoth!" cried the aardvark dad. "You probably won't see another one of those again."

"Oooooooooooh!" cried the kids sadly.

Sid gestured toward the kids to prove his point. "See," he said to Manny.

The aardvark dad glanced at his kids fondly, and then did a double take. Something was amiss! He began counting heads. He counted again. "Where's James!?" he cried.

James was still back at the pool where the giant ice boulder had crashed. He was leaning over to take a drink of water when a scary face popped out of the water right in front of him. It was the dim-witted Stu, who had been hiding underwater with his reed.

James screamed and sped off to catch up with his family.

Stu laughed and ducked back out of sight underwater. The two huge, sharp-toothed water reptiles that had thawed out of the ice boulder moved silently in the water underneath him. Not one of the other animals noticed when Stu's reed was suddenly yanked down under the surface.

Fast Tony appeared, looking for his assistant. "Stu? Where are you!?" he called.

Pftooot! One of the scaly monsters spat Stu's empty glyptodon shell out of the water. It landed upside down at Fast Tony's feet and spun around like a trash can cover.

"Ahhhhhhhhhhhhhhh! Stu!!!" yelled Fast Tony.

He picked up the shell and wiped away a tear. Then he considered the shell's potential value. His face brightened. "Folks, be the first in the valley to have your very own mobile home!" He rehearsed his new sales pitch as he jogged back to join the others.

CHAPTER 4

THE POSSUM FAMILY

All around the valley the glacial dams were weakening. The water park was already underwater, and throughout the entire valley, the ground was becoming soft and mushy. The animals pressed on toward the boat the vulture had spoken of, trying to avoid the sinkholes and falling debris.

Manny, Sid, and Diego followed behind, and Sid serenaded them with his silvery sloth voice. "Some day . . . when you've gone extinct . . . When you make a stink . . ."

"Shut up, Sid," grumbled Manny.

"Okay . . ." Sid switched to a perkier tune. "Stop, hey, what's that sound? All the mammoths are in the ground."

"Stop singing, Sid!" shouted Manny.

Sid kept pestering him. "Where have all the mammoths gone?" he sang.

Manny glowered at him. "Sid! If I fall on you again, I think this time I can kill you!"

"Okay, someone doesn't like the classics."

Manny stopped and gazed at multiple reflections of his face in the dripping icicles on the branches of a tree. "What if you're right?" he asked Sid. "What if I *am* the last mammoth?"

"You have us, big guy," said Sid.

"Not your most persuasive argument," said Diego.

Suddenly Manny's ears perked up. Could it be? Was that a familiar trumpeting sound he heard in the distance?

Diego heard it too. "Mammoths?"

"I knew I couldn't be the last one!" cried Manny joyfully. "I felt it in my gut!" He grabbed Sid, plunked him on his back, and charged through the forest, with Diego galloping close behind.

"Whoa! Whoa! Whoa! You're gonna get . . ." Sid ducked to avoid crashing into the low-hanging branches.

"Extinct!?" shouted Manny, plowing down bushes and small trees in his path.

Sid crouched against Manny's back like a jockey in the final stretch of the big race. "And he's coming around the corner," he cried. "He's up by a couple of fifths. And he's ahead by a tusk! Oh, and he's beating Diego as Diego's coming around the corner and . . . whoooooa!!!"

Manny screeched to a stop, and Sid was catapulted through the air. He landed on his face and slid through the mud.

"Ow, ow, ow!" he cried. The trumpet sounded again just inches from his face. He looked up to see a wide-angle view of a bear's rear end. It was Cholly the chalicotherium with a bad case of gas!

"Sorry, my stomach hates me," said Cholly sheepishly.

The trumpet sounded again.

Diego coughed and sputtered in disgust.

"Ew! Well, don't that put the stink in extinction," quipped Sid. "Whew, nasty!"

Manny turned away in despair, his last glimmer of hope extinguished.

"Manny?" called Sid, worried.

"I need to be alone for a while," said Manny sadly. "You go on ahead. I'll catch up."

Sid and Diego hated to see their friend suffering.

"One truly is the loneliest number," Sid said with a sigh.

As he and Diego walked away, a barrage of pebbles began whizzing toward them. "Ow, ow, ow!" they cried, flinching and dodging and ducking.

Diego looked over his shoulder and spied two possums, Eddie and Crash, hanging from a branch by their tails. They each had one of Fast Tony's dried-out reeds, and they were using them like peashooters.

"Hey!" shouted Diego.

Crash laughed. "These work great!"

Whap! He hit the big saber-tooth again.

"Cool!" cried Eddie.

Diego roared and leaped toward them.

The possum brothers jumped down from the tree and dove into a nearby burrow.

"Whoa! Missed me! Missed me! Now you gotta kiss me!" chanted Eddie.

"I'll get 'em!" cried Sid, diving head first into the hole.

Crash popped up out of a hole nearby, studied Sid's rear end, and inquired, "Which end is up?"

"I'd hide that head, too," said Eddie. He went under and popped his head out of the burrow's exit.

Sid sprinted after Eddie. Too late! Eddie dove back down and popped up again out of another hole.

Crash sprang out of yet another hole behind them. "Hey, ugly," he taunted. Sid had poked his head down in the hole looking for Eddie, and his butt was up in the air again. The perfect target! Crash shot another pebble.

"Ow! I gotta sit on that!" cried Sid, lunging at the shooter.

The two possums vanished and popped up again in different holes. They took aim and started pelting Sid with pebbles again.

Diego came up behind them and said, "Boo!"

"Waaaah!" cried the possums, quickly shooting at him and ducking back underground.

Sid gritted his teeth. "Okay, I'm going in!"

But before he could reach the hole, the possums stretched their tails across the ground and tied them together. Sid tripped over the makeshift rope and landed on Diego.

Up and down the possums went, with sloth and saber-tooth in hot pursuit. Finally, they heard Crash call out, "Over here!"

The two friends sprang toward him at once and collided, head-to-head, just as the wily possum disappeared down the hole again.

"Ow!" said Sid, rubbing his noggin.

Diego let out a frustrated sigh.

"Surrender?" asked Crash.

"Never!" cried Sid and Diego.

There was a long pause while Crash and Eddie stayed hidden underground. Sid and Diego looked at each other, wondering if the game was over. Suddenly Crash and Eddie sprang out of the ground and pelted them with a rain of pebbles as the possums somersaulted over their heads like gymnasts.

Sid and Diego made a lunge for them, but the two possums darted out of reach and ran up a nearby hill, laughing.

Diego and Sid collapsed on the ground in exhaustion.

"If anyone asks, there were fifty of them. And they were rattlesnakes," puffed Diego.

"Here, kitty, kitty!" taunted Eddie.

"Big mistake, you miscreants!" roared Diego.

"Miscreants?" Crash mocked.

"Uh, they're *possums*, Diego," corrected Sid.

Diego rolled his eyes.

From their hilltop refuge, Crash and Eddie began making chicken noises at them.

"Rrrrrrrrr." The saber-tooth sprang after them, with the slightly slower sloth right behind him.

Completely oblivious to the Whack-a-Possum game going on in the meadow, Manny stood forlornly on the riverbank gazing into the water. "I guess it's just you and me now," he said to his reflection. In his own lonely visage, he could see the faces of the wife and young son he had lost.

But his sad memories were interrupted by the

sound of a large branch cracking in the tree above. Suddenly an enormous shape plummeted down and stopped just before it hit the ground. There, right before his eyes, was another mammoth bobbing up and down as if she were hanging at the end of a bungee cord!

"Ah!" Manny gasped at the outlandish sight.

"Whoa!" cried the mammoth as the branch gave way, and she crashed to the ground.

"I knew it!" cried Manny. "I knew I wasn't the only one!"

"Me, too!" cried the mammoth. "Everyone falls out of the tree every now and then. They just don't admit it."

"Wait, what?" asked Manny.

"Some of us have a tough time holding onto branches. I mean, it's not like we're bats or something. We don't have wings to keep us up."

Manny looked at the mammoth, more perplexed than ever. "And you were in the tree because . . ."

"Oh, I was just looking for my brothers," she said. "They are always getting into trouble."

"Brothers!?" cried Manny. "You mean there are others?"

"Oh, sure. There are lots of us," she said.

"Where!?" cried Manny.

"Oh, I don't know . . . everywhere? Under rocks, in holes in the ground. Usually we come out at night so birds don't carry us off."

Manny was wondering what in the world she was talking about, when suddenly her "brothers" burst out of the bushes shouting: "Help! Ellie! Help!" They ducked behind her.

Diego and Sid leapt out of the bushes close behind them.

When they saw Manny face-to-face with Ellie, they stopped in their tracks.

"Well, shave me down and call me a mole rat!" exclaimed Sid. "You found another mammoth."

"Where?" asked Ellie. "I thought mammoths were extinct." She looked around anxiously until she realized everyone was staring at her.

"What are you looking at me for?"

"Maybe because you are a mammoth?" asked Manny.

"Me?" she asked. "Don't be ridiculous. I'm not a mammoth, I'm a possum."

Manny, Sid, and Diego stared at her blankly.

"Right. Good one," said Manny. "And I'm a newt."

He pointed to Diego. "And this is my friend, the badger. And my other friend," he pointed to Sid, "the platypus."

"Why do I gotta be the platypus?" complained Sid. "Make him the platypus."

"You're making fun of me," said Ellie sadly.

"No, no . . . well, yes," said Manny. "But I thought you were joking."

Crash stepped up to them, putting on his toughest gunslinger attitude. "These guys giving you trouble, Sis?"

"*Sis!?*" cried Manny.

"That's right. These are my brothers," said Ellie. She pointed to Crash and said, "possum," and then to Eddie and said, "possum." Finally she pointed to herself. "Possum. See?"

Manny leaned over and whispered to Sid, "I don't think her tree goes all the way to the top branch."

"Manny, brink of extinction's a bad time to get picky," noted Sid. His face brightened. "Hey, she should come with us!"

"Are you insane?" cried Manny. "No way!"

"Okay." Sid turned to Ellie. "Manny wants me

to ask you if you'd like to escape the flood with us."

"Wha—?" Manny sputtered in confusion.

But the possum brothers didn't want anything to do with Sid and his pals.

"Let me have a word with my brothers," said Ellie in a dignified way. She took them aside. "Look, we'll never make it out in time if we only travel at night. These guys can protect us out in the open. What do you say?"

"I'd rather be roadkill," cried Crash.

"I'd rather grow hair on my tail!" cried Eddie.

At the same time, Manny was arguing with Sid and Diego.

"Why did you invite them?" asked Manny irritably.

"Because you might be the only two mammoths left on earth," cried Sid.

"He has a point," said Diego. "This could be your last chance for a family."

"I'm sorry. When did I join the dating service?" said Manny.

Ellie returned with Crash and Eddie trailing behind her, grumbling. Ellie addressed Manny and his pals with a haughty air, "My brothers and I would be delighted to come with you."

"If you treat us nicely," said Crash, scowling at Diego.

Diego leaned menacingly toward Crash and bared his teeth.

"That there," stammered Crash, "that's the total opposite of nice."

"Maybe we'll have ourselves a little snack before we hit the road," crooned Diego.

"You want a piece of us?" cried Eddie. "Let's go, Crash!"

The two possums jumped on Diego and Sid, and the four of them swirled into a chaotic ball of punching and biting and scratching.

Crash paused for a second and lifted his head from the fray. "You know the best part? We're carrying diseases."

"Ew!" Sid and Diego jumped back and yelled.

Eddie and Crash hissed and spat at them.

"Here's a little plague, Fuzzface," cried Crash.

All around them the huge glacial dams cracked and boomed. Chunks of ice came crashing down.

The pumped-up furballs stopped and held their breath. It seemed like the whole world was falling down on top of them!

"Okay, thanks to Sid, we're now traveling together and, like it or not, we're going to be one big happy family," declared Manny. "I'll be the daddy, Ellie will be the mommy, and Diego will be the uncle who eats the kids who get on my nerves."

No one made a peep in objection.

"Now let's move it before the ground falls out from under our feet!" cried Manny.

Ellie eyed him, interested. "Hmmm," she said. "I thought fat guys were supposed to be jolly."

"I'm not fat," said Manny. "It's the fur that makes me look big. It's poofy."

"He's fat," she said to her brothers decisively as they scampered up onto her broad back for the long trek.

CHAPTER 5

LAST OF THE SPECIES

"**F**olks, escaping the flood is the perfect time to shed those unsightly pounds, with Fast Tony's Disaster Diet." Fast Tony's endless sales pitch droned on as terrified animals made their way over piles of loose debris and around treacherous rock slides.

The animals were so busy trying to escape the oncoming flood that nobody gave Fast Tony the time of day. Fast Tony spotted a large ox coming his way.

"You, ma'am! You look like a big, fat, hairy beast. How'd you like to lose a ton or two, eh?" Fast Tony said in his sales pitch voice.

"Would I ever!" exclaimed the female ox.

"Don't listen to him, Vera. You're already thin as a twig," her husband said.

The female ox smiled at her husband, and the pair continued on toward the boat with the rest of the animals.

"Oh, I also have the perfect cure for your eye-sight, my blind friend!" Fast Tony called after the ox.

As he scanned the horizon, he saw Manny and Diego in the distance. This time the fast-talking hawker decided to move his act to another corner of the herd before the annoying heavyweights arrived.

The possums kept under cover, scurrying from bush to tree. Ellie tried to camouflage her massive bulk with a few twigs and branches.

Manny rolled his eyes, watching her try to hide behind a tree that was way thinner than she was. "We'll never make it at this pace," he said to Sid and Diego. "Ellie, you can lose the camouflage. You're safe!"

"Okay!" called Ellie. But she checked with her brothers just to be sure. "Crash, Eddie, you two go scope it out."

They peeked out from behind the leaves.

"Whatcha got?" asked Crash.

"Perimeter looks to be all clear, Capt'n," replied Eddie.

"Roger that. One-niner over."

"Mmm, roger over, victor . . . ," Eddie teased.

Crash whacked him in the head.

"Ow!" cried Eddie.

Crash began to laugh, but Eddie grabbed him by the throat.

"Guys!" cried Ellie.

"All clear!" shouted Crash.

Finally Ellie dared to step out from behind the tree. Crash and Eddie tumbled out of the branches beside her. But just as they emerged from under cover, Eddie spotted something in the sky overhead.

He pointed. *"Hawk!!!"*

Crash and Eddie fell to the ground, motionless. Ellie dropped to the ground, too.

Manny peered down at her and asked, "What are you doing?"

"Playing dead," she replied.

"Manny, why don't you do that?" asked Sid.

"Because I am a *mammoth*!"

Ellie opened one eye. "Is he gone?"

"You're safe," replied Manny. "Get up."

"Whew," breathed Ellie. "If you weren't here, that hawk would've swooped down and snatched me up for dinner. That's how Cousin Wilton went."

Sid and Diego looked at each other in disbelief.

Ellie was still reeling from her narrow escape. "Boy, I really feel for you," she said to Manny. "I do. I can't even imagine what it'd be like to be the last one of your species."

Manny gestured toward her. "I'm not the last one."

"Oh, you brave, brave soul. That's right, don't give up hope," she sympathized, not getting his drift.

"Ellie," said Manny with a sigh. "Look at our footprints."

She looked down and saw Eddie and Crash's little footprints circling their big round ones.

Manny pointed to her footprints. "They're the same shape as mine," he observed.

Ellie peered at them suspiciously. "How do I know those aren't yours?"

Manny thought a moment. "Well, then, look at our shadows."

Ellie looked at their twin silhouettes on the ground.

"We match," said Manny.

She studied the two shadows and struggled to figure out what it might mean. Suddenly her face brightened. "You're right. They're the same!"

Manny beamed, triumphant.

"You must be part possum!" she cried.

"You wish!" exclaimed Crash haughtily.

Manny was about to say more, but another huge ice boulder came crashing down from one of the glaciers. Hawks and vultures were the least of their problems! The whole valley was quickly turning into one wide lake littered with rocks and giant ice floes. The travelers hurried on, crossing the water from ice floe to ice floe.

Eddie and Crash were having a blast, slipping and gliding like a couple of ice skaters. But Diego was tense. "Will you cut it out?" he snapped.

"Awww, c'mon, blubber-toothed tiger. Have some fun!" taunted Crash.

"Can't you see the ice is thin enough without you two wearing it down?" fretted Diego.

Everyone looked at the ice floe they were standing on. Diego was right.

"The ice may be thin, but it's strong enough to hold a ten-ton mammoth and a nine-ton possum," said Sid. "I even brought my rock collection." He held out a pile of pebbles to show Diego.

"Get rid of those!" growled the saber-tooth, paw-slapping them out of his hand into the water.

"My feldspar!" whined Sid.

They hurried on across the ice, trying to step lightly.

"I've got a really bad feeling about this," said Ellie. "My possum sense is tingling."

Manny chuckled. "Possum sense . . . there's no such thing."

But at that very moment, two immense shadowy shapes were sweeping past them under the ice.

Oblivious to the danger, Eddie shouted for joy, "Land ho!"

Before they could take another step, one of the menacing monsters, Maelstrom, burst through the ice, sending everyone careening off the floe.

"Mammal overboard!" cried Sid as he flew through the air.

Diego was spinning around on a small piece of ice, gripping it with his claws and hanging on for dear life.

Crash and Eddie spotted their sister lying unconscious on another floe. They made a dash for her. Crash pulled one of her eyelids up. "C'mon, sister!" he shouted. "If you play dead, you'll be dead!"

She roused herself and stood. But as she peered into the water she saw a terrifying sight: Sid was paddling as fast as he could toward Diego, with the immense, sharp-toothed Maelstrom swimming right behind him!

"Diego, help!" panted Sid.

But Diego was too petrified to even bat an eyelid.

Sid reached up and grabbed a hold of one of Diego's stiff, motionless legs and hauled himself up onto the ice floe. But the water reptile was zooming in fast. Sid had to think of something quick, or they would both be swallowed up together in the reptile's giant maw.

Suddenly a look of inspiration crossed his face. "This might sting a little," he cried, chomping down on Diego's tail.

"Owooooo!" Diego howled.

Sid darted away, with a furious Diego following after him.

Just in the nick of time! Behind them ice crashed and crunched. They turned to see Maelstrom bursting out of the water and completely obliterating their ice floe with one bite.

Trapped on another chunk of ice, Manny looked on in disbelief as Sid and Diego sprinted toward shore, with Maelstrom mashing through the ice after them.

Wham! The other water monster, Cretaceous, suddenly leapt out of the ice, snapping his powerful jaws shut just a hairbreadth from Manny's nose.

Manny watched, terrified, as the monster circled around and came up again on the other side. Suddenly, all Manny could see was a mouthful of razor-sharp teeth coming at him. *Clonk!* The powerful jaws slammed shut.

Argh! Cretaceous was stunned. His mouth had clamped shut on Manny's hard ivory tusks. Manny shook the reptile off and Cretaceous fell back into the water. Manny stumbled and nearly toppled into the water himself. But his floe had moved close enough to shore. He pushed off the ice and bounded to safety. Diego and Sid stepped up beside him and peered at the mammoth-sized bite mark in Manny's ice floe.

Cretaceous and Maelstrom glared at them from the water, sizing them up for their next attack. Then they silently slithered away into the murky depths.

Sid's eyes were about to pop out of his head in disbelief. "What . . . in the animal kingdom . . . was *that!?*"

"As if drowning wasn't enough," shuddered Diego.

Ellie and the possums joined them on shore.

"That was the bravest thing I've ever seen," said Ellie.

Manny swelled with pride. "It was nothing," he said humbly. "Really, I . . ."

"Oh, it's not a compliment," she declared. "To a possum, bravery is just dumb."

"Yeah," agreed Crash, "we're spineless."

"Lily-livered," added Eddie.

"Maybe mammoths are going extinct because they put themselves in danger too often. Maybe you should run away more," suggested Ellie.

Manny could not believe what he was hearing. "Good tip. Thanks for the advice."

"Happy to help." Ellie sauntered ahead with her possum brothers.

Manny turned to Sid and Diego. "Do you believe her? 'Bravery is just dumb. Maybe you should run away more,'" he mimicked her. "She's infuriating and stubborn and narrow-minded!"

"Yep. She's a mammoth alright," quipped Sid. "Yooooou like her."

"I do not!" Manny stomped away.

"Don't worry, your secret's safe with me!" Sid called out after him. He turned to Diego. "Oh, and so is yours."

"What secret?" cried Diego.

"The one where you can't swim."

"That's ridiculous."

"Fine," sighed Sid. "But we're living in a melting world, buddy. You're gonna have to face your fear sooner or later."

Diego knew Sid was right. They could see the water rising even as they stood there on the shore. The two pals hurried to catch up with Manny and Ellie and the possums.

Ellie and her brothers were pushing logs up to the crest of a hill.

"Almost there," said Crash. "Ugh! Okay, ready, Eddie!?"

"Let's roll!" cried Eddie. He and Eddie let their big hollow log roll down the hill. As it picked up momentum, the two possums jumped inside and tumbled with it like two sneakers in a dryer at the Laundromat.

Manny, Sid, and Diego watched, speechless.

As if the possums' log trick was not weird enough, a moment later Ellie zoomed past them, riding atop her own log like a lumberjack in a fast river.

"No breaks! Gotta roll!" she cried. "Meet'cha at the other end!"

"So, Sid," said Manny, nodding in Ellie's direction. "You think she's the girl for me?"

"Yeah! She's tons of fun and you're no fun at all." Sid put on a sappy face. "She completes you, Manny."

At the bottom of the hill, Crash and Eddie's log banged to a stop against a big rock. They crawled out and staggered around dizzily, trying to give each other a high five but slamming into one another instead.

Crash climbed up a young sapling. "Hey,

Manny!" he cried. "Can you pull this tree back and shoot me into the pond?"

"No," said Manny. He walked past the possum without even giving him a glance.

"How do you expect to impress Ellie with that attitude?" asked Sid.

"I don't want to impress her," replied Manny.

"Then why are you trying so hard to convince her she's a mammoth?"

"Because that's what she is!" shouted Manny. "I don't care if she thinks she's a possum! You can't be two things!"

"Au contraire, Man-fered," replied Sid. "Tell that to the mole hog, chicken hawk, or turtledove!"

"Manny, he's never going to let up on you," said Diego. "It'll be easier on all of us if you just go with it."

Manny gritted his molars, took a deep breath to steel himself, and went back to Crash. "So what do you want me to do?"

"Just pull the tree back and shoot me into the pond," answered Crash.

Manny looked from tree to pond. "I don't know . . ."

"If you're too lame to do it, we can get Ellie," cried Crash.

"No, no," said Manny. "I can do it. I can do it." He pulled the tree back with his trunk.

Crash assumed a takeoff position and licked a finger to test the wind. "Farther. Farther. Farther," he ordered.

"Have you done this before?" asked Manny.

"Only a million times," sighed Crash. "Farther. Farther. Perfect. Now . . . FIRE!"

Manny did as he was told. *Sprong!* The tree snapped upright and Crash went soaring through the air.

"I can flyyyyyy!" he sang. *"I believe I can fly. . . ."*

Smash! He whammed headfirst into an oak tree and plopped to the ground like a sack of potatoes. Acorns rained down around him.

Everyone ran to his side in a panic. Crash was curled up in a ball, his legs twitching.

"Crash! Crash? Crash!?" screamed Eddie.

Ellie came back to see what was wrong. "What happened?"

"Manny shot him out of a tree," tattled Eddie.

She looked at Manny crossly. "What's wrong with you?"

Manny shrugged. "He said he could do it."

"And you listened to him?"

"Yeah, but . . ."

They heard Crash moan. Eddie fell dramatically to his knees and held his brother in his arms. "Crash! Whatever you do, don't go into the light!"

"Uh, can I help?" asked Manny earnestly.

"You've done enough," cried Ellie. "Just go. Please."

Manny glared at Sid and Diego. "Are you happy now?"

They felt terrible.

"Crash, Crash, don't leave me! Who's gonna watch my back?" wailed Eddie. "Who's gonna be my wingman of mayhem? Who's gonna roll in that dung patch with me?"

At the words "dung patch" one of Crash's eyes sprang open. "Wait. My legs. I can stand," he muttered.

"He can stand!" cried Eddie.

"I can run!" cried Crash.

"He can run! It's a miracle!" shouted Eddie.

Whooping and hollering, they bounced off to the dung patch, dove in, and began to roll.

Manny and his friends looked at Ellie.

She shrugged and giggled weakly. "What can I say? They're boys. They make my life a little adventure."

Then she stormed over to her brothers, glowering. "You guys are so dead—thanks for embarrassing me! Come back here!"

"Ow! Ohh! Not the face!" the possums cried dramatically, as their big sister loomed over them, threatening to give them both a good thrashing.

Manny, Sid, and Diego winced.

CHAPTER 6

SACRED MAMMOTH GROUNDS

Manny watched as Ellie, Crash, and Eddie played with each other, having a fun family moment. His eyes glazed over as he tilted his head to the side.

"Manny?" asked Diego.

Manny snapped out of his daze and turned to face Sid and Diego. He picked up a tree that was in his way and swung it, almost beheading Sid and Diego.

"You were thinking about your family again, weren't you?" Diego asked.

Manny picked up another tree and moved it as Sid and Diego jumped over it to avoid getting hit again. Sid stood on one of the trees as Manny lifted it up.

"You never talk about her. What was she like?" Sid asked.

Manny flinched at Sid's question. Sid fell and hung upside down in Manny's face.

"She was the best part of me. She never saw me, but every night I watched her put our son to sleep. The only thing more beautiful than the way she looked at me was the way she looked at him. And I got to see that every day," Manny said with a sigh.

"You can have that again," Sid said gently.

"No, Sid, I can't," Manny responded.

"Okay, but think about it: If you let this chance go, you're letting your whole species go! And that's just selfish!" Sid yelled.

Manny stormed off after tossing the tree—with Sid still in it—out of his way.

* * *

As the sun began to set that evening, Crash and Eddie led the way through a ruined forest. The ground had become mushy, and all the trees were tipped over at odd angles. The nimble possums climbed over them and ducked under them like kids on a playground. Ellie tried to follow, but she was soon wedged under a fallen tree.

Behind her she could see Manny trudging through the mess, using his trunk to uproot the trees in his way and toss them aside. "Need help?" he asked as he caught up to her.

"Nope," she replied. "Just catching my breath."

"You're stuck," said Manny.

Ellie scowled. "I am not."

Manny sighed. "Alright, then, let's go." He lumbered off again through the swampy forest.

"I can't. I'm stuck," admitted Ellie.

Manny lifted the tree and freed her.

Suddenly Ellie fell silent and all of her senses snapped alert. She felt as if mysterious but familiar voices were calling to her. She started moving forward, spellbound.

Curious, Manny followed her into a beautiful, wide-open meadow. The setting sun shone behind the trees in deep red and purple hues, lighting them up like stained glass. It was the most magical place he had ever seen.

The tops of the willow trees swayed in the gentle breeze, taking on the shapes of different mammoths. Ellie stopped in front of one of the trees. The sun flashed on its branches, lighting up its familiar form.

"I *know* this place," she gasped.

In a flash, she was looking at herself as a youngster. There was snow on the ground, and she was running around frantically searching for something. She was all alone, shivering in the sharp biting wind. She saw herself huddle up, crying and afraid, under the shelter of a tree. It was this tree! The very same tree she was looking at right now.

And there, hanging from the branch above, she could see a possum. Ellie saw her infant self wipe away her tears as she looked up into the kindly mama possum's eyes. Two little baby possums peeked out at her from behind their mother. Her brothers!

Ellie realized she was seeing a memory from long ago.

Manny saw her ashen expression and watched her as she looked down and, for the first time, really noticed her footprint next to his. She studied them for a while, then carefully lifted her foot and placed it in his footprint. She looked up at Manny with tears in her eyes.

"A mammoth never forgets," he told her kindly.

"You know, deep down I always knew I was different," Ellie sighed. "I was always a little bigger than the other possum kids—okay, *a lot bigger*. I could barely fit on my mother's back."

"There's nothing wrong with being big-boned," Manny encouraged her.

Ellie looked at him, surprised. "That's what *she* used to say. And it always made me feel better. But then I saw you. I'd never seen anyone who looked like me before. Now I understand why possum boys never found me appealing."

"That's too bad. Because as far as mammoths go, you're . . . uh . . . you know . . . ," Manny stammered.

"What?" asked Ellie.

"Um . . . well . . . a-a-attractive."

"Really?" Ellie perked up and smiled.

"Yeah." Manny relaxed a little.

"What else?" asked Ellie.

"Huh? Well . . . there's . . . your . . . uh . . ." Manny groped for words. Any words!

Ellie stared at him.

" . . . butt?"

"What about it?" demanded Ellie.

"It's . . . big?"

Ellie smiled. "You're just saying that."

"No, I mean it. It's huge!"

"That's really sweet," she sighed happily.

"Biggest darned butt I've ever seen."

She chuckled. "What a crazy day. This morning I woke up a possum and now I'm a mammoth."

Manny smiled, delighted.

"C'mon! Let's go uproot something!" she cried. "I wanna see what this new mammoth body can do!"

"But you've always had that body!" cried Manny.

Ellie had already raced halfway down the hill. Manny shrugged and hurried off after her.

At the bottom of the hill, Sid was setting up camp so everyone could settle in for a much-needed rest.

He lit the campfire, and countless little eyes gleamed at him from the surrounding darkness. Diego stepped into the circle of light, and the eyes quickly vanished.

"Boy, Manny sure took a big leap with Ellie," said Sid. "Faced his fear and dove right in—splash! Kind of brave, huh?"

"I wouldn't know," replied Diego. "Sabers don't feel fear."

"Oh, c'mon. All animals feel fear. It's what separates us from, say . . . rocks!" cried Sid. "Rocks have no fear. And they sink."

"What are you getting at, Sid?" growled Diego.

"It may surprise you to know that I, too, have experienced fear," said Sid.

"No, *you?*" said Diego sarcastically.

"Yes," said Sid. "As impossible as it seems, the sloth has natural enemies that would like to 'harm' or 'kill' us."

"Gee, I wonder why."

"Jealously, mostly," said Sid breezily. "The point is: Fear is natural."

"Fear is for prey," declared Diego, and he stormed away from the annoying sloth.

"Well, then you are letting the water make you its prey," cried Sid.

The idea hit Diego like a splash of cold water in the face. He stopped in his tracks and stared back at his friend.

"Look," Sid continued, "most animals can swim as babies. You gotta jump in. . . ."

He leapt into a bush and crouched in diving position. "Trust your instincts. Attack the water! *Grrrrrrrr*." He dove out of the bush and crawled across a log. "And for a tiger, it's just like crawling on your belly to stalk cute, innocent, helpless prey. . . ."

Diego turned away, and Sid lowered himself down right next to him on a dangling vine. He swung around on the vine as if he were swimming through the air.

"Then *claw, kick. Claw, kick*. I'm stalking the prey," he instructed Diego. He lifted his head to demonstrate: "Up for a breath. Now I look over my shoulder to see if I'm being followed." He made imaginary swimming strokes with his arms. "Now, I'm stalking . . . I'm stalking . . . I'm breathing . . . I'm stalking . . ."

The flood
is coming!

Manny, Sid, and
Diego must get to
the other side of
the Valley.

Diego reached up with his big claws and sliced the vine.

"I'm falling . . . ," cried Sid. *Splat!* He hit the ground face first.

Diego loomed over him. "Correction. You're sinking. Kind of like a rock."

At the same time, Manny was doing a different kind of sinking all his own. As he and Ellie approached the campsite, Ellie continued to marvel over her new identity. "Our species is so powerful! But, then, we're gentle, too."

She nudged him with her shoulder and nearly knocked him over. "Whoops, sorry. Don't know my own strength yet."

"And Ellie, do you realize that now we have a chance to save our species?" asked Manny.

"How are we going to do that?" she asked, puzzled.

He was afraid to look her in the eye. "Well, you know . . . ," he stammered.

Ellie thought for a second. "Did you just . . . ?"

"No, I didn't mean . . ."

"Unbelievable!" she cried. "I'm not a mammoth for five minutes and you're hitting on me?"

"I wasn't saying . . . Not right now!" Manny tried to backpedal. "I was just saying, it's our responsibility. . . ."

"What!?" she fumed.

"That came out wrong."

"Responsibility?" she demanded. "Just doing your duty—is that it? Ready to make the ultimate sacrifice to save your species?"

"No, no," Manny spluttered. "Uh . . . you're very pretty. But we just met. I wasn't . . ."

"Well, I've got some news for you," Ellie declared. "You're not saving the species tonight or any night!"

She stormed off to find her brothers, and Manny slunk over to the campfire next to Sid.

"So, how was your big date?" Sid asked.

"Um, not bad," lied Manny.

A few minutes later, Ellie stomped into camp with her brothers on her back. "Okay, let's go," she ordered Manny and his pals. "We traveled with you all day; now you're coming with us at night."

"But we can't see at night," whined Manny.

"Then enjoy the flood," said Ellie, stomping off.

Eddie threw Manny a disgusted glance. "I can't even look at him."

"He's extinct to me," cried Crash. "Pervert!"

Sid and Diego rose and extinguished the fire.

Sid looked at Manny and shook his head. "Makin' friends. Everywhere you go, just makin' friends."

Manny shrugged sheepishly, as the three pals lined up obediently to follow Ellie out into the night.

CHAPTER 7

TOPPLING ROCKS

As the night wore on, a thick fog rolled in, and Diego took the lead while the possums used their agility and keen night vision to help them avoid hazards. Manny and Sid brought up the rear, stubbing their toes on rocks and running into stumps and branches.

Manny struggled to catch up with Ellie.

"I thought we could walk together," he suggested.

"Crash, ask the mammoth why he thought that?" said Ellie sarcastically.

"She said she thinks you're a jerk and to go away," interpreted Crash.

"She didn't say . . . !" Manny stumbled over a rock. "Ouch!" he cried. "Argh!" He stopped himself and tried to speak calmly to Ellie. "Look, maybe if we spend more time . . ."

Whack! He hit his head on a low hanging branch.

"Tell him that I need a little personal space right now," snapped Ellie.

"She said go jump in a lake and that possums rule," cried Crash.

"I can hear her, you know," whined Manny, rubbing his head.

"What do you want, a medal?" asked Crash.

Manny shook his head.

Suddenly they heard Diego shouting, *"Stop moving!"* Through the dense fog, they had accidentally walked right onto a high pile of tippy rocks!

The animals gasped and shuffled to a stop. They felt the whole rock formation shifting under their feet. It was tilting from side to side, like a seesaw, between two cliffs.

"Ahhhhhhhhhhhhhh!" they screamed.

"Let's get off this thing!" cried Ellie. She and the possums ran back toward one of the cliffs, but the formation leaned and crashed against the cliff wall, sending the wall crumbling down, and leaving them all standing on a high, swaying island of rock.

"Aaaaaieeeee!" screamed Crash and Eddie. They leaped into each other's arms, causing the formation to wobble even more.

"Everybody relax! Stop moving!" commanded Diego.

They froze, and the rocks stopped swaying.

"Thank you," said Diego.

With that, the rock under theirs collapsed, and Diego and Manny fell to a rock below. Ellie and Sid and the possums were still clinging to the larger rock above, but it began to tilt.

"Manny, Ellie—lock trunks!" Diego ordered.

The two mammoths eyed each other warily.

"Now!" shouted Diego.

Manny reached his trunk up and locked it with Ellie's. The big rock tipped backward. The mammoths anchored their feet and held on for dear life, together just barely keeping the rock in balance.

Diego eyed the ledge opposite them and thought fast. "Eddie! Crash!" he cried. "Use your tails. Jump down and swing the rock back and forth to reach that ledge."

Eddie and Crash peered over the edge of their rock. It was a long, long way to the ground and a long distance to the next ledge.

"Funny. Now what's your *real* plan?" quipped Crash.

"Just do what I say!" cried Diego.

Crash and Eddie turned and bade each other a teary-eyed farewell.

"Go now!" shouted Diego.

The possum brothers screamed and jumped. Eddie wrapped his tail around the rock and, holding Crash by his hands, swung like a trapeze artist toward the ledge, while Manny and Ellie hung on.

"I . . . uh . . . I'm sorry if what I said earlier offended you," Manny stammered.

"What do you mean *if* it offended me?" demanded Ellie. She pulled back, and the rocks began to tip.

"*That* it offended her!" yelled Crash, desperate to help them patch things up before it was too late. "*That* it offended her."

"I mean, *that*. *That* it offended you," corrected Manny.

Ellie inched closer.

"You just overreacted, that's all," blundered Manny.

"What?" She pulled back again and the rocks wobbled.

"Take it back!" cried Crash. "There are other lives at stake here!"

Sid scratched his head. "Wait a minute, he's got a point."

The rocks shook.

"He's got nothin'!" yelled Crash.

"It was a misunderstanding," said Sid.

"It was insensitive!" shouted Eddie.

The rocks were teetering precariously.

"Manny, apologize now!" growled Diego through clenched teeth.

"Why me?" whined Manny. "She overreacted."

The rocks pitched back and forth on the brink of collapse.

"This wouldn't be happening if Dad had let her date Cousin Vinnie," said Eddie to Crash.

"Just apologize!" yelled Diego.

"Okay, I'm sorry!" cried Ellie.

"What!?" Everyone turned to her in surprise.

The rocks stopped wobbling and swaying.

"He's right," she said quietly. "I overreacted."

"You mean you . . ." Manny started.

"Stop!" cried Diego. "Not another word or I'll push you over myself."

Manny buttoned his mammoth lips. The acrobatic possums were finally able to swing their rock over to the solid ledge. They hopped off to safety, followed by Sid, then Ellie and Manny. The last one off, Diego leaped toward them just as the entire rock formation began to give way behind him. Manny and Ellie caught him with their trunks as the rock formation collapsed to the ground in a great thundering avalanche.

Ellie glanced at Manny, exhausted but triumphant. "I guess we finally did something right together," she said.

Manny stopped and looked at her.

"Hey, don't mind me!" called Diego. "Just hanging off the edge of the cliff here!"

Manny and Ellie flipped him up to safety, and everyone heaved a sigh of relief.

When the fog lifted, they made their way down

the hillside, and Sid built a campfire at the base of the cliff. Soon everyone had flopped down around it to sleep. "Remember the good ol' days?" Sid asked Diego, as he adjusted the rock beneath him.

"Which good ol' days?" Diego asked sleepily.

"Oh, you know," Sid replied. "Back when the trees went up and down and the ground stayed *under* our feet."

"Those were good days. Possums were possums and mammoths were mammoths . . ." Diego trailed off. "We should get some sleep."

"Yeah, tomorrow's the day the vulture said we're all gonna die," Sid agreed. And with that, he laid his head on the rock and drifted off to sleep.

Manny stirred and peeked up at Ellie as she lifted her sleeping brothers and hung them by their tails from a branch, kissed them each good night, and smoothed down the ruffled fur on their heads.

Then she climbed the tree and wrapped her mammoth tail around a branch to sleep next to them. Her weight bent the limb down so far that her trunk was lying on the ground. Manny fell back asleep, smiling.

CHAPTER 8

SID THE FIRE-GOD

In the early morning hours, as the eastern sun was just touching the valley with its rose-colored light, the rock that Sid was sleeping on suddenly rose up off the ground and began moving away from the campfire.

He opened one eye. Either the whole landscape was moving or he was!

"Wait a minute," he said. He looked down over the side of the rock, only to discover that it was being carried off by a peppy team of mini-sloths.

"Uhhh . . . can I help you?" Sid addressed them.

As they approached a clearing, Sid could see a whole tribe of mini-sloths waiting for them.

He stared at them, and the sloths stared googly-eyed back at him. They all dropped to their knees in unison. One reverent mini-sloth held up a large melon.

"For me?" asked Sid.

Before Sid could grab it, the mini-sloth shoved it into Sid's mouth, while another handed him a flower.

He sniffed it. *"Aaaaachoooo!"* He sneezed melon all over one of the minis in the crowd, and she went into raptures of joy.

Two young mini-sloths placed a crown of flowers on Sid's head and turned him so he was facing a gigantic fifty-foot-high sculpture of . . . himself!

"Who is your decorator? I mean, this is fabulous!" cried Sid. "Do my thighs look that fat?"

The minis dumped him off his rock with a thud and handed him two small stones. The chief of the tribe solemnly pointed to the rocks in Sid's hand.

"Fire-god. Rocks," she declared.

"Oh . . . I'm the *Fire-god*. Riiiiight," said Sid. "Well, it's about time someone recognized my true potential." Sid gazed out over the admiring crowd. "Okay! Fire-god rocks!"

He smashed the rocks together and sparks flew, igniting the bubbling tar pit below the statue. Jets of fire exploded up into the sky.

The mini-sloths let out a triumphant war cry.

Sid struck a victory pose, and the ladies sighed and swooned. He strutted across the stage like a rock star, with plumes of fire shooting up all around him.

A special sloth brigade formed a mini pyramid and lifted Sid up to the pinnacle. Sid waved and blew kisses. The sloths danced and spun through a dazzling display of pyrotechnics until the grand finale when Sid felt them wrapping a long vine around his body and pulling it tight.

"This is either really good or really bad," he muttered.

The sloths stopped before a deep crevasse, with a seething, bubbling tar pit at the bottom.

Sid panicked. "No, no, no. Me Fire-god," he

cried. "Why kill Fire-god? A thousand years bad juju for killing Fire-god!"

"Superheated rock from the earth's core is surging into the crust, melting ice built up over thousands of years, causing great floods," said the chief.

Sid stared at her, impressed. "You are a very advanced race. Together we can look for a solution."

"We have one," she declared. "Sacrifice the Fire-god!"

"That's not very scientific!" shouted Sid.

"Worth a shot," she shrugged.

The mini-sloths pitched him into the pit.

"Aahhhhhhhhhh!" Sid screamed.

The minis cheered. They lifted their little arms and danced.

Sid felt his eyelashes burn off in the intense heat as he plummeted down to his fiery doom. But like a natural bungee cord, the vine caught and held him just before he hit the bottom. He grabbed hold of something—a giant dinosaur bone! All around him dinosaur skeletons gleamed in the flaming mist. As he let go, the bungee vine sprang up, sending Sid rocketing up out of the pit.

The minis cheered even louder! Then down he plummeted again, this time getting tangled in a big pile of bones.

With one last hurrah, the minis declared the Fire-god dead.

But at that moment a huge dinosaur skeleton sprang up out of the pit, flew through the air, and crashed on top of the statue of Sid. The minis saw Sid trapped inside the skeleton.

"Bad juju!!" cried a baby mini.

The crowd screamed in terror. Bats flew out of the statue's nose, and Sid used one of the bones to bat at them. Suddenly the whole monument began to crumble, and the sloths scurried for cover.

Sid went flying into a deep ravine. He tumbled down the side and landed, hard, on the ground.

By the time the sun was fully up, the mammals' campsite was getting soggy.

Diego leapt up from his sleep. "Water. Water! Water!" Before he even knew what he was doing, he'd jumped up on Manny's back.

Manny woke up, startled, and they tipped over

against the possums' tree. Crash, Eddie, and Ellie splashed down, one, two, three.

Eddie rolled his eyes at his brother. "Crash, I told you not to drink before bed."

"I didn't do this!" cried Crash. "At least not all of it."

"What's happening?" asked Ellie.

"We overslept," said Manny. "We need to move."

"What if we're the last creatures left alive!?" cried Eddie. "We'll have to repopulate the earth!"

"How?" asked Crash. "Everyone's either a dude or our sister."

Suddenly, they heard a rustling in the reeds, and Sid appeared, stumbling and half-asleep.

"Oh, hi, Manny. Wow. What a night. You'll never guess what happened to me."

"I'm gonna go out on a limb and say you were sleepwalking," said Diego.

"Oh, no, no, no. I was kidnapped by a tribe of mini-sloths," replied Sid.

"That was gonna be my second guess," said Diego dryly.

"They worshipped me! Sure, they tossed me into a flaming tar pit. But they worshipped me!" gushed Sid.

"Sid, you were dreaming," said Manny. "C'mon."

"I wasn't dreaming! "Why is it so hard to believe that I was kidnapped and worshipped by a tribe of mini-sloths?"

"You had us at kidnapped," Diego said.

"You lost us at worshipped," Manny chimed in.

"But I'm telling you! I was kidnapped. I was worshipped."

But his pals had already resumed their journey.

CHAPTER 9

CROSSING THE GEYSER FIELD

As the glaciers melted and receded, they created a wide, wet landscape filled with immense boulders and piles of rocky debris. An enormous web of new streams meandered this way and that. Old rivers had swollen into wide lakes and waterfalls spilled from nearly every cliff.

The whole landscape had changed, but with a

little luck the exhausted group managed to make it to the top of a hill where they finally spied the floating thing the creepy vulture had described. It was a huge sequoia boat perched high atop a distant mountain. They could see many different kinds of animals streaming toward it from all directions.

"There it is," stated Ellie, numbly.

"We made it!" cheered Eddie, tossing a big handful of mud in the air. It plopped down on Crash's head. Crash picked up another handful and slung it at his brother. Within seconds they were all laughing and tossing mudballs at each other in celebration.

Manny and Ellie reached down into the mud for more ammo and accidentally touched trunks. They looked up into each other's eyes and were surprised by the deep connection they felt. Their hearts melted like the glaciers. Ellie flashed Manny a mischievous grin and Manny read her mind. They scooped up big heaps of mud and . . . *Rat-tat-tat-tat!* They shot quick rounds at Crash and Eddie, Sid, and Diego.

Before the pals could retaliate, the whole hillside they were standing on suddenly gave way with a big *whoosh*.

"Ahhhhhhhhhhhhhhhh!" they cried as they were carried down by the mudslide and landed—*Splat!*—in a big hole, each one of them sticking out of the mud at a different angle, like a handful of tossed pickup sticks.

Sid, Crash, and Eddie hauled themselves out of the hole first.

"We raced the water and lost," Diego said.

Before them lay a treacherous minefield pocked with steaming vents. Every now and then, seemingly without any rhyme or reason, one of the vents would blow, sending boiling hot water spouting high into the air.

"Oh, it's just a little water and steam," Sid said. "How bad could it be?"

The gunslinger vulture swooped down and landed in front of them. "There's no escape! You're going to be boiled alive! It will be an instant of pain that feels like an . . ." Before the vulture could finish its sentence, a geyser went off and blasted the bird to smithereens. Feathers drifted down around them like snow.

"Now *that's* a visual aid," gulped Sid.

Manny stepped forward in an attempt to investigate the situation. A geyser blew up right next him.

"Manny, get back. It's a minefield out there," warned Diego.

Manny stepped back and surveyed the land before him, as geysers blew up all around the group.

One by one the giant redwoods began to lose their grip and fall.

"Crash! I'm too young to die!" cried Eddie.

"Actually, we have really short life spans, so you're kinda due," said Crash unhelpfully.

"Ahhhhhhhhhhhhh!" screamed Eddie.

"You had to find out sooner or later," said Crash. "Might as well be from me."

"There's only one way to go. Straight through," said Manny.

"No, we'd like to keep the fur on our bodies, thank you. We'll head back and go around. That's safer," said Ellie.

"There's no time. The dam'll burst before we make it. We'll drown," said Manny.

He walked up to Ellie and stared her right in the face.

"We go through this, we'll get blown to bits!" she exclaimed.

As the two fought, water started to seep into the ground, covering the animals' feet. Blasts of steam and water continued to shoot up all around them. Diego and Sid exchanged nervous glances.

"We go forward!" screamed Manny.

"We go back!" screamed Ellie.

"Forward!"

"Back!"

Manny stood up straight to tower over Ellie, hoping to assert some authority. Ellie responded by straightening herself up as well, standing eye to eye with Manny. The tension was rising as the group stood still, scared to move for fear of walking right into an active geyser.

"Can I say something?" interjected Diego.

"NO!" screamed Ellie and Manny in unison.

"You are so stubborn and hard-headed," Manny said.

"Well, I guess that proves it! I *am* a mammoth!" Ellie shouted back.

"Then act like one!" Manny said.

The two mammoths stood face-to-face, not saying a word. They were both breathing heavily, neither one willing to back down.

"Well, maybe it's time we go our separate ways," said Ellie, breaking the silence.

"No. We stay together as a group," Manny asserted.

"We're not *your* responsibility!" said Ellie as she turned to leave. She started to walk, and the possums followed close behind her.

Manny hung his head in frustration and breathed a mammoth sigh. He walked away angrily with his group, as Ellie walked away with hers.

Manny marched right into the geyser field, without hesitating to plan out a route. Sid and Diego just followed right behind him, trying to stay as close as possible to their leader. Geysers shot up all around them.

"Drowning sounds like a much gentler way to go. Blown to bits is so . . . sudden," Sid whispered to Diego.

Sid continued to shriek at random moments while geysers shot up all around him. As the herd made their way through the geysers, Manny, lost in his frustration and anger, kept on walking. Sid stopped to tiptoe around the geysers, and after a few minutes at this pace, Manny was way ahead of him.

Manny marched on, paying no attention to the explosions surrounding him, when a geyser erupted, blowing him backwards. Stunned, he listened to the voices repeating in his head.

"Kids, look! The last mammoth!"

"I just heard you're going extinct!"

"Bravery is just dumb. . . ."

"You can't be two things."

"She thinks you're a jerk. Go away."

"Where's your big happy family?"

"What if I am the last mammoth?"

"What's wrong with you? What's wrong with you?"

Diego ran up to Manny and snapped him out of his stupor.

"C'mon, Manny! Let's go!" Diego shouted.

The group ran out of the geyser field into safe territory. They were almost at the boat.

CHAPTER 10

THE BOAT

At the boat, the scene was chaotic. Hordes of animals pushed and shoved and spat and hissed at one another. Two vultures sat hunched above it all on a big dead branch, making announcements.

"Do *not* leave your children unattended," said one ominously.

"All unattended children will be eaten," declared the other.

Manny, Sid, and Diego pressed through the crowd, searching for Ellie and the possums.

Manny asked everyone he passed: "Have you seen a mammoth?" The animals shook their heads.

He leaned down to address a tapir dad. "Hey, buddy. Have you seen a mammoth?"

"I sure have!" cried the tapir. "Big as life!"

"Where?" cried Manny.

"I'm looking at him," said the tapir.

"Not me!" cried Manny.

The tapir leaned over to his wife and whispered, "Poor guy doesn't know he's a mammoth." He looked up and cried "Hey! I see another one!"

"Where? Where?" cried Manny.

"Sorry, it's you again," joked the tapir.

Diego whisked poor Manny away. "Maybe she's already onboard," he said.

A loud, thundering rumble came from across the long valley. Everyone turned toward it at once. The rumble echoed off the sides of the valley, increasing steadily in volume and intensity. The terrified animals pushed and shoved to get near the boat.

An officious secretary bird named Gustav manned the entrance. Two big rhinos stood behind him like linebackers.

"Animals! Please!" he cried. "Rub your bellies, roll over on your backs, do whatever you do to calm yourselves down!"

A huge flock of birds whooshed overhead, heading out of the dangerous valley at top speed.

Manny and Diego tried to push past Gustav's beefy bodyguards.

"Let us through," cried Manny. "We have to find someone."

"A possum," added Diego, "about eleven feet tall."

Gustav pinned them with his beady eye. "You must have missed the preboarding announcement," he said, snippily repeating it for their benefit: "At this time we are only boarding animals with *mates.*"

"Mates?" cried Sid and Diego.

The little Scrat, who had just stepped up with an armload of acorns, slunk away, disappointed.

Two frizzy-furred females immediately began to quarrel over a scrawny male mammal of the same species.

"He's mine!" cried one.

"I saw him first!" cried the other.

Sid looked at Gustav. "What if you don't have a mate?"

"Then you can travel standby," replied Gustav.

"What's standby travel?" asked Diego.

"You stand by, we travel," quipped the bird.

"Isn't there anyone else we can talk to?" huffed an aardvark.

"Yeah, Mother Nature will be here any moment to field questions," said Gustav.

"Hey, what about you?" cried Manny. "You don't have a mate!"

"Yes," snapped Gustav, "but I have power. The rule does not apply to me."

But while they argued, the glacier at the end of the valley had begun creaking and booming and cracking and splintering under the tremendous pressure of the water behind it. The ground shook. The animals jostled and squashed one another in panic.

Already high above them, on the steep icy wall of the valley, the rejected, dejected little Scrat was pounding his acorns into the ice, one by one, creating his very own escape ladder.

CHAPTER 11

SAVING ELLIE

Ellie had discovered a shortcut to the boat and was carrying her brothers toward it when suddenly they heard the ominous rumble of a landslide. A boulder crashed down and landed inches from Ellie's trunk. Then more rocks rained down on them, trapping them inside a cave. Ellie tried to shove a boulder out of the cave's opening, but it was too heavy, and more debris was accumulating behind it by the second.

"You guys gotta go," she told her brothers.

"No way! We're not leaving you!" cried Eddie.

"I'm not asking," she declared, stuffing him and Crash through the one remaining crack in the opening.

"Ellie! No!" they cried.

Crash pointed to the boat nearby.

"Let's go get help!" Eddie agreed.

"Stay here!" Crash shouted to Ellie.

Duh, she thought.

Boom! At that moment, the entire ice dam exploded. Cretaceous and Maelstrom, the horrible water reptiles, were swept up in the cresting wave. The rushing, churning flood pounded through the valley, obliterating everything. Balancing rocks toppled like marbles in the ocean. Geysers became underwater jets. In a matter of seconds, everything was changed.

As the waves roared and crashed through the mountains, Manny shoved Gustav aside and announced: "At this time, we are now boarding *everyone!*"

"Yeeeeeaaaahhhhhh!" Hundreds of panicked animals scrambled onto the boat.

Suddenly Crash and Eddie's voices rang out loudly above the roar of the crowd. Manny looked around and spotted the two possums elbowing their way toward him.

"Manny!" cried Crash, breathless.

"It's Ellie!" shouted Eddie.

"She's trapped in a cave!" exclaimed Crash.

At once Manny raced off the boat, down the hill, and across a rickety ice bridge toward the cave. Manny crossed first, with the possums sprinting to catch up. But just as the possums hit the bridge, a giant wave swept it away, dumping them all into the rising water. Manny swam straight for the cave while Eddie and Crash grabbed onto a tree.

Manny turned and saw his friends in trouble.

"Go! Save our sister!" cried Crash.

Sid noticed the possums clinging to the tree.

"I'll save you!" he offered. He dove off the ledge of the boat and promptly clonked his head on a block of ice, knocking himself out.

"Great, who's gonna save him?" wondered Crash, using his tail to try and fish Sid out of the water.

Diego looked at Sid. He looked at the possums clinging to their tree for dear life. If he didn't save them, no one would. He mustered all his saber-toothed courage and crouched to spring. "Okay. Jump in . . . *now!*" he ordered himself.

But nothing happened. His legs refused to move. "C'mon, 'fraidy cat. Big breath and . . . *jump!*"

Still he remained frozen in place, coiled to spring, eyes closed.

"Trust your instincts," Diego said to himself, remembering Sid's words. "Attack the water. I am not your prey. . . . I am not your prey. . . ."

He leaped! *"Ahhhhhhhhh!"*

The big cat splashed into the water, all four paws flailing. The possums saw him go down. They shook their heads, imagining the worst, when suddenly Diego burst up through the surface of the water gasping for breath.

He wasn't sinking! *"Attack the water. I'm stalking the prey. Claw, kick. Claw, kick. Even babies can do it. Claw, kick, claw, kick. I'm stalking the prey!"* he repeated to himself.

It was working! Diego grabbed Eddie. But Crash and Sid floated away from him. He placed Eddie onto his head and paddled after Crash and Sid. He helped Crash onto his head alongside Eddie, but Sid was sinking before his eyes. He took a deep breath and dove for him. After a few seconds he rose up out of the water, the two possums still clinging to his head. Sid was hanging limply from his mouth.

Diego set Sid gently down on the ice and then collapsed next to him, breathless and sputtering. Sid eyes popped open. "You did it, buddy. You kicked the water's butt!"

"Nothin' to it," rumbled Diego. "Most animals can swim as babies."

"Not tigers. I left that part out."

Meanwhile, the water level in Ellie's cave had risen nearly to the top of her raised trunk. Her head bumped against the ceiling. More and more water kept rushing in! Manny grabbed a tree and jammed it into the small cave opening from where Crash and Eddie had escaped. He pushed and pulled on the tree trunk, trying to dislodge the boulder. The water was nearly over his head now, and the big rock wasn't budging.

Just as the water was about to reach the ceiling inside the cave, cutting off Ellie's air completely, she managed to stick her trunk through the opening for another breath. But soon her eyes were bulging and her cheeks were turning blue. She couldn't hold her breath much longer.

Manny continued to try and pry the boulder out with the tree trunk. He came up for air for a second and was instantly pulled underwater by Cretaceous. The villainous reptile was back! Sid, Diego, and the possums watched in horror. There was nothing they could do.

"Manny," Sid called out.

Manny tried to hold on to the tree trunk and pull himself above the water again, but Cretaceous had him by the tail. Manny lost his grip and disappeared under the water again. Maelstrom joined his buddy and the two of them zeroed in for an underwater attack. They banged and bit and fin-smacked Manny from all angles.

Wham! Manny landed a deft kick on Maelstrom's monstrous head. It dazed the reptile just long enough for Manny to swim free. He popped up and gasped for air. He paddled against the current, trying to keep his head above water.

Back underwater, Manny could see the cave with

the log still jammed in the opening. He swam toward it, the nasty water reptiles right behind him. Just as they were about to ram into Manny with all their strength, he swam out of the way, leaving them to smash into the tree, dislodging the boulder. The giant boulder rolled on top of Cretaceous and Maelstrom, pushing them far beneath the surface.

Ellie floated out of the cave, unconscious. Manny carried her gently to shore where Sid, Diego, and the possums helped him pull her out of the water.

"Ellie!" Crash and Eddie exclaimed.

"You're okay!"

"We thought we'd never see you again!"

Ellie opened her eyes and looked up at a smiling Manny. She rose to her feet to stand beside him. The water continued to rise all around them, isolating the group on a small island of dry land.

Scaling the valley wall above them, Scrat pounded his last acorn into the ice. A treacherous crack spread down through the entire glacier. The huge ice mountain split. Scrat clung to both sides as the fissure slowly widened. Water began to gush below him through the growing gap. He struggled to keep his grip on the groaning ice, trying desperately to pull it back together.

Whoa! His paws slipped, and little Scrat tumbled through the air.

"Ahhhhhhhhoooooooooooooooo!" The other animals heard little Scrat wail as he splashed down into the churning water and disappeared.

The water around the herd continued to drain through the gap in the glacier. Suddenly the whole valley was dry. They were saved!

A great hurrah erupted from the deck of the escape boat, which was now resting on the valley floor.

"Everyone, we have reached our final destination!" declared Gustav. "Please exit in an orderly fashion!"

He was flattened like a pancake in the ensuing stampede.

"Or do it your way," he groaned.

Sid, surrounded by kids exiting the boat, turned to Diego and said, "I'm thinking about starting a swim school: Sid's squids." But Sid was soon interrupted. He turned around and saw his kidnappers—the tribe of mini-sloths! He screamed and hid behind Diego.

"All hail Fire-god!" A female mini-sloth cried.

The mini-sloths bowed. Sid stepped out from behind Diego.

"Uh . . . hi?" he said uncertainly.

"Hi-hi-hi-hi-hi-hi . . ." the mini-sloths repeated.

"Fire-god avert flood. Join us, O Great and Noble Flaming One!" the female mini-sloth said.

Sid started toward them, but Diego stopped him. He couldn't let his friend go without a fight. "Your choice of gods is wise beyond your size. But his herd needs him. He is the gooey, sticky substance that holds us together. We would be nothing without him."

The mini-sloths bowed again and turned to go.

"You mean it?" Sid asked, smiling at Diego.

Sid threw his arms around him. "Yuck, Sid. Get off me! That doesn't mean I want to touch you," Diego growled.

Just then, Manny, Ellie, and the possums walked over.

"Don't ask," Diego said, still trying to push Sid off of him. But the group did not have time to think about Sid and Diego. Suddenly, they heard a trumpeting sound.

CHAPTER 12

THE REUNION

Manny looked up at the sound and did a double take. A majestic herd of mammoths was coming over the hilltop! Manny and Ellie gazed at them in wonder and amazement. They leaned close to each other, their eyes welling up with tears. The herd made a circle around them.

The mammoths cheered and trumpeted at the

good fortune of finding the two lonely stragglers. "Well, we're not the last ones anymore," Ellie said.

"So, you want to go with them?" Manny asked.

"Well, I *am* a mammoth," she said. "I should probably be *with* a mammoth, don't you think?"

"Yeah, unless," said Manny hesitantly.

"Unless . . . what?" Ellie asked.

The mammoths made their trumpet call, signaling that the time had come to be on their way.

Manny was at a loss for words. "I just want to say . . . I need to tell you . . . ," he struggled. "I hope you find everything you're looking for."

Ellie's face dropped with disappointment. "Oh," she replied tersely. "Okay. You, too."

"Good-bye, Ellie."

"Good-bye."

Ellie turned to go. She looked back over her shoulder. But Manny just stood there, stunned and silent.

Sadly, she lifted the possums onto her back and joined the herd.

Diego and Sid stepped up to him.

"Manny," Sid started. "You've come a long way since we've met, and I'll take full credit for that. But you need to let go of the past so you can have a future."

"Go after her," said Diego.

"It's okay. We'll always be here for you," said Sid.

"I'll keep in touch," said Manny as he slowly moved toward the herd.

"Yeah, yeah, yeah," said Diego, shooing him along. "You're a good friend. Now go on, scat."

"Our Manny's growing up," said Sid proudly.

Manny began to walk a little faster. Soon he was running!

"Ellie!" he shouted.

Deep in the middle of the herd, Ellie's ears perked up. Had she just heard something? Crash and Eddie stood on tiptoe on her back and craned their necks for a view. Ellie turned and walked against the traffic to the back of the herd. She didn't see anything.

Then suddenly Manny appeared from above, hanging upside down from a tree branch by his tail! He was so heavy, the tree was bowed to the ground, close to the breaking point.

"Ellie, I don't want us to be together because we *have* to," said Manny. "I want us to be together because we *want* to. And I want to be with you,

Ellie . . . so what do you say?"

Ellie gave Manny a look of great affection.

In his excitement, Manny fell out of the tree—
kerplunk!

"You're possum enough for me," Ellie smiled.

Crash and Eddie laughed and wiped away each
other's tears of joy.

"Hey, Diego," said Sid. "It's just you and me now.
Two bachelors, knockin' about the wild. Woo-hoo!"

"Fine, but I'm not going to carry you," growled
the big cat. "I still have my pride."

"Oh c'mon, buddy. For old time's sake," pleaded Sid.

"I'll carry him," a deep voice announced. It was
Manny. He swooped Sid off his feet and set him
high on his back.

"But your herd's leaving," said Diego.

"We are *now*," declared Manny.

"Lead the way, Mr. Übertracker!" cried Sid to
Diego.

Crash and Eddie settled happily on Ellie's familiar
back, and the small herd of miscellaneous oddballs
headed off through a breathtaking new rock canyon
into the rosy sunset.

"Hey, Manny," said Sid. "Look at this canyon.

The stone's so yellow."

"Hmmm, that's not yellow stone," said Manny. "It's more like . . . ochre."

"Suddenly you're the color expert?" cried Sid. "That's yellow stone, Manny! Yellow stone."

EPILOGUE

High up above them, Scrat popped his head over a white fluffy cloud and looked around. A celestial choir of dodos sang behind him. But when he turned to see who was there, they disappeared. He backed up slowly and bumped into something. It was the Pearly Gates! They swung open, and the little rodent entered Scrat Heaven.

A treasure trove of acorns lay before him, bathed in warm, glowing light. Scrat backstroked through the sea of acorns in pure bliss. He looked up and saw the biggest nut he had ever laid eyes on—the Master Nut! He dropped the smaller nuts he was holding and raced toward it. But just as he was about to reach it . . .

Woosh! What was happening!? He felt himself being sucked out of the gates. He grabbed the gates and hung on, desperate to stay. But one by one his little claws lost their grip. It was no use! He was being yanked back down through the sky.

His spirit reunited with his lifeless body on the ground. He felt something wet and sloppy on his lips! Argh! It was that sloth, performing mouth-to-mouth resuscitation! Scrat coughed up water and sputtered back to life.

Sid's eyes lit up with delight. "I saved you, little buddy!"

Scrat glowered at him and wiped the sloth slobber from his snout. He looked around, desperate for Scrat Heaven. He whimpered and pounded the earth in frustration.

Sid stood by helplessly and scratched his head, as the feisty little Scrat shook his fist and charged at him accusingly.

"Calm down, calm down . . . I saved you, little buddy, remember?" asked Sid. "I . . . Ow, ow, ow . . . !"